ROCK RAIDERS

Written by Alan Grant
Storyboards by Robin Smith
Illustrated by LEGO Media International, Denmark
Managing Editor: Sarah Camburn
Art Editor: Stephen Scanlan

First published in the United States in 2000 by LEGO Systems, Inc.
555 Taylor Road, P. O. Box 1600, Enfield, CT 06083-1600

© 2000 LEGO Group

The LEGO ® symbol is a registered trademark of the LEGO Group.

2 4 6 8 10 9 7 5 3 1

ISBN 1903 276055

Join the LEGO Community
www.LEGO.com

Printed in Singapore on behalf of Imago

Meet the team!

NAME: Docs
RANK: Commander

Docs is a very learned man, renowned for his skills in locating precious energy crystals and LEGO ore. Unlike Axle, Docs always assesses a situation before making a decision, though sometimes he thinks a little too much.

NAME: Axle
RANK: Midshipman

Three times 'LEGO World Racing Champion', Axle's ability to handle anything with wheels is second to none. Axle is a bit impulsive and tends to dive headfirst into a situation without thinking.

NAME: Sparks
RANK: Midshipman

Sparks is curious about anything mechanical or electrical and is forever taking things apart and putting them back together. Unfortunately, he is also the clumsiest member of the team!

NAME: Bandit
RANK: Sub-Lieutenant

Bandit is happiest on water, sailing on underground lakes or riding rapids. An expert navigator, he always knows where he is. Bandit does not stand any tomfoolery and if things aren't going well he will grumble for hours.

NAME: Jet
RANK: Flight Lieutenant

Jet's piloting skills are legendary. Ready for any challenge she always approaches her missions with a level head. Jet will never shirk a difficult task and has great problem-solving skills.

NAME: Chief
RANK: Captain

Chief is the oldest and most experienced member of the team. He is calm in any situation and has the experience to solve almost any problem. He is modest and wise.

Chapter 1: PLANET OF THE MONSTERS

WOULDN'T YOU JUST KNOW IT? WE WERE ONLY THREE DAYS FROM HOME, LOOKING FORWARD TO A HARD-EARNED VACATION, WHEN EVERY ALARM ON THE SHIP WENT CRAZY -

Meteor storm! Strap in, you Rock Raiders!

This could be a bumpy ride!

We're being sucked in!

Hold on for all you're worth!

We've come out the other side. We're safe!

And I didn't spill a drop!

SPARKS MAY BE THE BEST ENGINEER IN SPACE - BUT HE'S ALSO THE CLUMSIEST!

Oops!

A WORMHOLE IS LIKE A SHORTCUT THROUGH SPACE. THE ONLY PROBLEM IS, YOU NEVER KNOW WHERE YOU'LL END UP.

TRY BUILDING A SPACESHIP OUT OF LEGO BRICKS

I don't recognize any of these stars, Chief. I figure we've been transported to another galaxy.

We lost a lot of energy. This could be serious, Docs!

Maybe not, sir. My geo-locators say this planet's a prime source of power crystals.

THERE WAS ONLY ONE WAY TO FIND OUT FOR SURE – THE ROCK RAIDERS HAD TO TELEPORT DOWN TO INVESTIGATE-

Scanners indicate that the planet's low on oxygen. You'll need to build purifiers.

Be careful – there's no saying what you'll encounter down there!

Good luck!

OUR HOVER SCOUTS REAPPEARED DEEP INSIDE A MASSIVE CAVERN-

Wow! What a size!

There's no way that this can be natural! It's been carved out of solid rock by someone... or something!

I'm landing to take a closer look!

Remember what the captain said, Axle, be careful!

Don't worry about me, Jet! I can look after myself!

FAMOUS LAST WORDS! AXLE'S A GREAT DRIVER, BUT HE TENDS TO BE A LITTLE HEADSTRONG-

Hey! This stuff's like superglue!

I'm stuck!

Suffering space rats! What the heck is that?

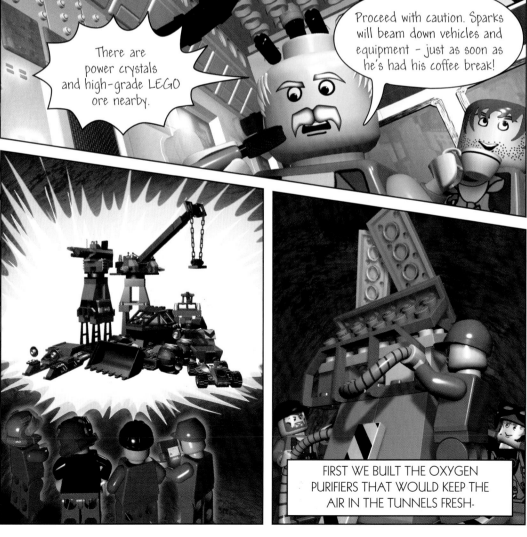

NEXT CAME THE ORE PROCESSING PLANT-

AND, SO THAT OUR GROUND TERRAIN VEHICLES COULD GET IN AND OUT EASILY, A BRIDGE OVER THE LAVA RIVER-

Look at me! I'm the king of the castle!

Watch you don't slip, Axle!

Yikes!

Chapter 2:
FIRE AND ICE

WE WORKED FOR TWO DAYS WITHOUT A BREAK, AND THE LEGO ORE AND ENERGY CRYSTALS BEGAN TO MOUNT UP.

DOCS ESTIMATED THAT WE'D HAVE ENOUGH TO POWER THE L.M.S. EXPLORER AND STILL HAVE PLENTY TO TAKE HOME AS CARGO. THAT IS IF SPARKS AND THE CHIEF COULD FIGURE OUT WHERE HOME WAS!

STILL, WE'D BEEN ON DOZENS OF EXPEDITIONS... AND CHIEF HAD NEVER LET US DOWN YET-

HAVE A GO AT BUILDING YOUR OWN ORE PROCESSING PLANT

How many of each of the following objects can you find? Turn to the last page of this book for the answers:

- boulders
- red lights
- wheels
- pickaxes

Look out, Bandit! Rockfall!

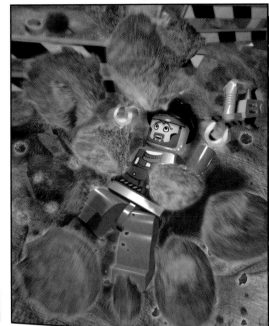

Hurry! We've got to get him out of there!

Here he is!

Are you okay, Bandit?

Say something!

Wh-where am I?

It won't be able to follow me in here, the opening is too small.

Incredible! It's walking through solid rock!

Keep away from me, you monster!

It's lost interest in me! All it wants is the power crystal!

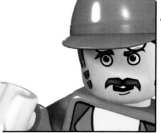

WE'D DISCOVERED THE UNDERGROUND LAKE ABOUT A MILE AWAY DOWN THE TUNNELS, AND THERE WAS NOTHING BANDIT LIKED SO MUCH AS EXPLORING IN HIS RAPID RIDER-

Docs calling Bandit! Be alert for rock monsters!

Don't worry about me, Docs! 'Careful' is my middle name!

'Grouchy' more like!

TRY BUILDING A LEGO RAPID RIDER

I heard that!

Jet! There's a lot of ice here. I'm moving closer to investigate.

It's like a glacier flowing into the lake.

No sign of any monsters, though.

Urk!

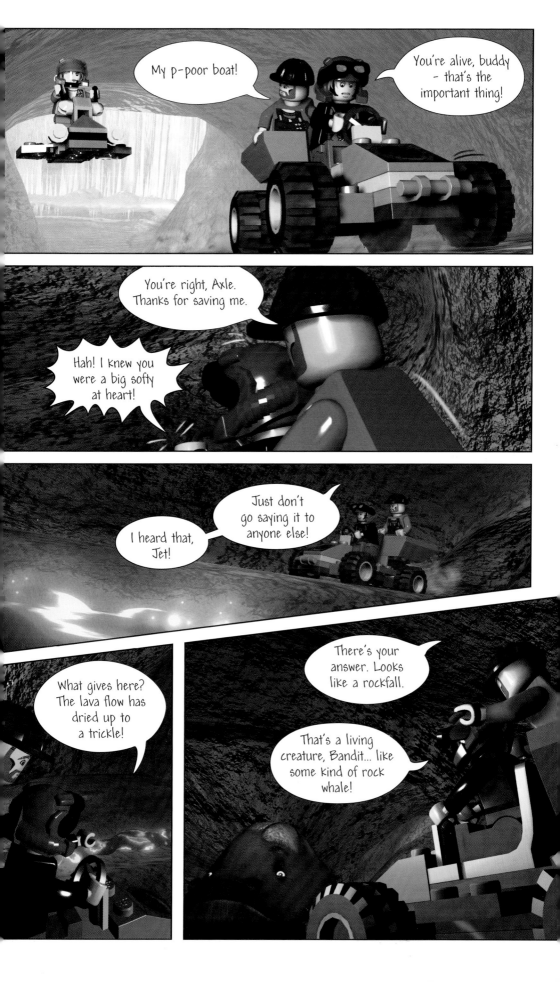

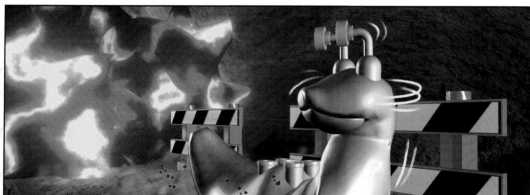

BLOCKED BY THE FALLING CEILING, THE LAVA HAD ONLY ONE WAY TO GO-

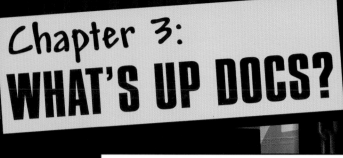

Chapter 3:
WHAT'S UP DOCS?

ROCKS FROM THE TUNNEL COLLAPSE HAD BEEN CAUGHT IN THE TELEPORT BEAM, CAUSING SERIOUS DAMAGE. BUT CHIEF'S NEWS WAS EVEN MORE GRIM-

Can't we teleport him back?

Bad news, Rock Raiders. Docs is missing!

His personal locator is still functioning, but all communication's gone dead!

How many of each of the following can you spot in this scene? Turn to the last page of this book for the answers:

- orange arrows
- yellow pipes
- pale green lights
- brown chains

BEFORE HE LEFT, DOCS HAD SET THE CHROME CRUSHER AND LOADER DOZER TO AUTOMATIC. THEY WERE STILL POUNDING AWAY AS BANDIT LEFT-

TRY BUILDING A LEGO GRANITE GRINDER

Too bad you drew the short straw. Axle. You have to stay behind on guard.

I'll use the time to make up some jokes.

THE GRANITE GRINDERS WEREN'T AS FAST AS HOVER SCOUTS, BUT THEY'D GIVE US MORE PROTECTION-

AND THEIR POWERFUL DRILLS MEANT THAT WE COULD TAKE SHORTCUTS-

Power crystals! That's a nice bonus!

BANDIT'S VOICE SEEMED TO ECHO DOWN THE TUNNEL FOR EVER BEFORE IT FINALLY DIED AWAY.

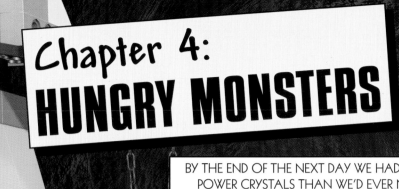

Chapter 4:
HUNGRY MONSTERS

BY THE END OF THE NEXT DAY WE HAD GATHERED MORE POWER CRYSTALS THAN WE'D EVER NEED. TRUST THE MONSTERS TO DECIDE THAT WAS THE TIME FOR THEM TO SETTLE THEIR DIFFERENCES AND TEAM UP WITH EACH OTHER!

Bad vibes, dudes!

The monsters are hungry... and it looks like feeding time!

How many of each of the following can you find in this scene? Turn to the final page for the answers:

- [ ] crystals
- [ ] ice monsters
- [ ] rock monsters

TRY BUILDING A LEGO ROCK MONSTER

Jet to LMS Explorer...

Beam us and all the crystals up, Sparks! We're in a tricky spot!

You and me both! This teleporter's proving more of a problem than I thought!

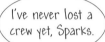

I've never lost a crew yet, Sparks.

Send me down!

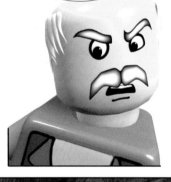

Aye, aye, sir!

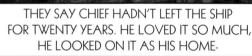

THEY SAY CHIEF HADN'T LEFT THE SHIP FOR TWENTY YEARS. HE LOVED IT SO MUCH, HE LOOKED ON IT AS HIS HOME-

BUT HE LEFT THAT DAY TO SAVE HIS TEAM-

You will not pass!

THE POWER UNLEASHED BY HIS PLASMA ARM WAS PHENOMENAL. I'VE HEARD HE HAD TO HAVE IT FITTED AFTER HE LOST HIS REAL ARM RESCUING 37 MINERS IN A CAVE-IN ON PLUTO-

BUT I DON'T KNOW ANYONE BRAVE ENOUGH TO ASK HIM IF IT'S TRUE-

Even he can't hold out forever! Sooner or later they'll break through – and we can kiss goodbye to all our crystals.

What the heck is keeping Sparks?

I just don't understand. It really ought to be working!

Would you believe it? I forgot to plug it in!

I DON'T KNOW WHAT HAPPENED TO THE MONSTERS AFTER WE LEFT. I'D LIKE TO THINK THEY TRIED TO RECLAIM THEIR LOST CIVILIZATION.

BUT THAT'S ONE QUESTION I GUESS I'LL NEVER HAVE ANSWERED.

That's a record haul of crystals, Docs. Everybody's going to get a fat bonus when we get home.

Talking about home, Chief...

Any idea how we're going to get there?

LET'S GET BUILDING

If you don't have the LEGO Rock Raider play sets, there's no need to fret. It's easy to build models that look pretty similar out of the LEGO bricks you do have at home. The models shown here are just our suggestions – yours can vary in any way you want, according to what you have at home – all you need is a little imagination!

TRANSPORT TRUCK
This nifty, easy-to-handle vehicle is useful for carrying around crystals and LEGO ore. Although limited in its use, it can be really speedy when handled by a skilled driver.

ROCK MONSTER
These huge creatures lie dormant within the walls and caves of the underground world. They survive by eating the energy crystals and guard their food jealously. Once you have built a rock monster, try building lava and ice monsters, too.

ORE PROCESSING PLANT

This is the nerve centre of all the Rock Raiders' activities. There is a high-powered crane to lift boulders on to the platform where the crystals and LEGO ore can be analyzed and extracted. New equipment can also be made here and damaged vehicles repaired. The plant also houses the teleportation platform.

GRANITE GRINDER

This is a powerful digger that can climb over difficult terrain using its long, agile legs. Don't forget to add powerful turbines to the back of the driller to power the single drill at the front.

RAPID RIDER

This is the only water-going vehicle in the Rock Raider fleet. It's fast and easy to handle, and is mainly used as one-man transport. There's a bucket on the back for transporting precious crystals and two powerful spotlights that can cast light over a wide area.

H.M.S. EXPLORER

This impressive mining ship is the pride and joy of the Rock Raider's Captain. Its reinforced exterior has been built to withstand the biggest of meteorite showers. It is equipped with all the latest technological gadgets to make it the speediest ship in the LEGO universe.

PICTURE HUNT ANSWERS
Chapter 2: 10 boulders, 16 red lights, 16 wheels, 4 pickaxes.
Chapter 3: 7 orange arrows, 8 yellow pipes, 11 pale green lights, 12 brown chains.
Chapter 4: 13 crystals, 26 ice monsters, 25 rock monsters.